Terriers and Tiaras
On Stage

Written by

ORCHARD

# Contents

Chapter 1

A Special Delivery

The sun was streaming through the windows of the Littlest Pet Shop as Blythe Baxter hung out with her favourite pals.

"What are you working on?" asked Zoe, a Cavalier King Charles spaniel with style to spare.

"I'm not sure yet," Blythe admitted.

She carefully
started shading
in her latest
fashion design –
a frilly skirt and
lacy scarf that
would be perfect
for a dog like Zoe.

"Well, you might
not know what it is, but I know that I love
it!" Zoe told her.

"Thanks, Zoe," Blythe said. "When my
new fabric arrives, it will be easier to
figure out if this design will work or not."

Ring-a-ling!

Everyone looked up as Lewis, the
postman, walked through the door.

"Ooh, maybe it's already here!" Zoe
said excitedly.

But all Lewis heard was *yip-yip-yip-yip!*

"Easy, girl," he said, glancing at Zoe. "I don't know what it is about dogs. They all seem to hate the postman."

Blythe tried to hide her smile. "I think she's just excited to see you."

Being able to communicate with animals was one of Blythe's many talents, and she was determined to keep it a secret. She couldn't imagine what would happen if people ever realised that all those yips, yowls, squawks, and meows were really words!

"Any packages for me today?" Blythe continued.

"Well, I'm not sure," Lewis said. "Are you expecting…a special delivery express package from 2 Cute Fabrics Incorporated?"

"Yes!" Blythe squealed.

Just then, Mrs Twombly, the owner

of the Littlest Pet Shop, returned from the stockroom. "I don't know, Blythe," she said. "We're running awfully low on Pampered Pet Gourmet Snacks and—"

At that moment, Mrs Twombly noticed Lewis. "Oh! Perfect timing! Is there a delivery from the Pampered Pet Company?"

"Several cases, ma'am," he told her. "If you'd just step outside to sign for delivery…"

While Blythe opened her package, Zoe took a peek at the rest of the post. "Hey, Blythe – what's that?"

"Looks like a postcard." Blythe started to read the note. When she gasped, all the pets turned to look at her.

"What is it? What's wrong?" Russell the hedgehog asked.

"Nothing's wrong," she said. "In fact, everything's perfect! Remember when the reality TV show *Terriers and Tiaras* filmed an episode in Downtown City?"

All the pets nodded. It had been one of the wildest weeks ever, especially when Zoe had begged Blythe to accompany her. Zoe felt like her dreams of being a reality TV star had finally come true! But it had turned out more like a nightmare. Zoe had decided that reality TV shows, with all their made-up drama and bad feelings, were not for her. When she quit, the other famous pooches had followed her lead. And they'd never been happier!

"Well, we've just received a postcard

from Philippa and
PS!" Blythe continued
excitedly.

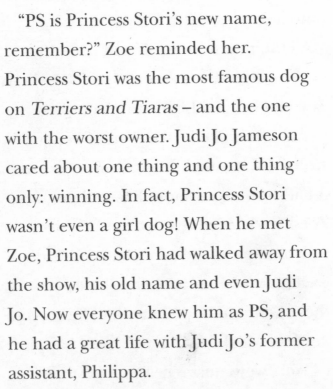

Minka, a mischievous
monkey and artist
extraordinaire, looked
confused. "PS?" she asked.

"PS is Princess Stori's new name,
remember?" Zoe reminded her.
Princess Stori was the most famous dog
on *Terriers and Tiaras* – and the one
with the worst owner. Judi Jo Jameson
cared about one thing and one thing
only: winning. In fact, Princess Stori
wasn't even a girl dog! When he met
Zoe, Princess Stori had walked away from
the show, his old name and even Judi
Jo. Now everyone knew him as PS, and
he had a great life with Judi Jo's former
assistant, Philippa.

Blythe held up the postcard.

"'Dear Blythe,'" she read. "'How are you? I have some exciting news. PS and I are taking a road trip…and we're going to stop in Downtown City! We can't wait to see you and Zoe! Love, Philippa.'"

Blythe turned the postcard over and showed the pets the back. "There's even a paw print from PS at the bottom," she added.

"A PS from PS!" joked Pepper.

Zoe flashed her most dazzling smile. "This is the best news ever!" she cried. "If only the rest of our *Terriers and Tiaras* pals could visit, too."

"That would be so cool," Blythe agreed. "Like a reunion!"

"You're a genius, Blythe!" Zoe cried.

"We simply have to invite Shea Butter and Sam UL, too!"

"That's a great idea, Zoe!" she replied.

"Wait a second…" Zoe had another brilliant thought. "Maybe we could do more than have a reunion. Maybe…we could put on a show!"

For the first time, Blythe's smile faded. "A…show?" she asked. "I don't know, Zoe. Don't you remember what happened last time?"

Everyone cringed a little – especially Blythe, who had served as Zoe's handler at the show. She had transformed into one of the most demanding, pushy dog-show mums of all time! Luckily, Blythe realised that she was going about it all wrong…and everybody could tell that Blythe never wanted to let a show affect her caring personality again!

"That won't happen this time," Zoe assured her. "This show will be about performing and sharing talents! And this time, everyone gets a chance to have their time to shine."

"Even me?" squeaked Sunil the mongoose. He wasn't quite sure if this was something he needed to worry about, but when it came to worrying, Sunil believed it was never too early to start.

"And me?" added Vinnie the gecko. Vinnie and Sunil were best friends, but Vinnie didn't spend much time worrying. He'd rather work on his dancing skills – and play with his pals.

"Everyone who wants to," Zoe declared.

"OK, I give in," Blythe said, smiling.

"On one condition. Zoe, I want you to be in charge of the show."

"Me?" Zoe asked in astonishment.

"I'm happy to make the costumes and help out, but if I'm in charge, I might start bossing everybody around again," Blythe explained. "So if you—"

"Yes, yes, yes!" Zoe cried excitedly. "Thank you, Blythe! I know I can do this. First, we'll need a place to have the show…"

"What about here?" suggested Penny Ling, a gentle, graceful panda.

"That might work," Zoe said. "Or maybe…the Pawza Hotel."

"Wonderful idea!" Sunil beamed. "Their new lounge is opening soon."

"Maybe we could even be the new lounge's opening night act!" Zoe cried.

"But I'm getting ahead of myself. First, we've got to invite everybody else. Blythe, would you email their owners for me?"

"On it!" Blythe replied.

TO: tanya.twitchel@paw.com, cindeanna.mellon@paw.com
CC: philippa@paw.com

SUBJECT: *Terriers and Tiaras* Reunion Show!

Hey, everybody! Exciting news – Philippa and PS will be visiting Downtown City, and we're hoping you can visit, too! It would be so great to have a *Terriers and Tiaras* reunion show, but it wouldn't be complete without you and your pups. We can even put on a show! LMK if you can come. See you soon (we hope!!!)

Love,
Blythe and your friends at the Littlest Pet Shop

Blythe tapped her phone to send the email to Sam UL's and Shea Butter's owners. "Now I'm going to call the Pawza Hotel to see if we can book our show," she announced.

Zoe was so excited she felt like dancing. The *Terriers and Tiaras* reunion show was officially happening.

And so it was time to get to work!

Chapter 2
The Perfect Poster

"We have to start practising now,"
Zoe told her friends. "PS, Sam UL and
Shea Butter have tons of experience.
We don't want to look silly next to the
professionals. Does anybody know which
talent they'd like to perform?"

"Maybe I could do a new routine with

my ribbon stick," Penny said.

"That sounds perfect!" Zoe exclaimed.

"People love to laugh," Pepper spoke up. "I've been practising my mime routine. There's a part where I pretend I'm being chased by a giant banana."

Zoe giggled. "Pepper, I love that idea – it sounds hilarious! Now, Vinnie and Sunil – what about you guys?"

Sunil popped his top hat on his head. "Magic, of course!" he cried. "I have a brand-new trick that's ready for the spotlight."

"I had a feeling you would," Zoe said. "How about you, Vinnie?"

"Hmm, a dance routine? I can show off my best moves."

"Great!" Zoe said. "Start practising

right away, my friends."

As Penny, Pepper, Sunil and Vinnie scurried off, Zoe realised that Russell and Minka were still there. "Oops! We can't forget about you two," she told them. "What do you want to do?"

Russell and Minka exchanged a glance.

"Um, Zoe, I'm not sure that being onstage is the best job for me," said Russell.

"But, Russell! When all the dogs walked off the show, you won the crown," Zoe reminded him.

"Yeah…well…once was enough," Russell said sheepishly. "But I still want to be a part of everything. Don't you need a helper? Blythe's making costumes, but what about building the set?"

"Oh!" Zoe exclaimed. "Of course. I didn't even think about the set. Thanks!

That's a great job for you!"

"And I can paint it!" Minka suggested. "And make some posters, too, so we can advertise the show."

"You two are the best," Zoe said.

"Big news, everybody," Blythe announced as she joined them. "The entertainment for the opening night of the Pawza Hotel's new lounge cancelled this morning. The manager was panicking about finding a replacement! He thinks your idea for a *Terriers and Tiaras* reunion show is fantastic!"

Suddenly Zoe had another idea. "Blythe!" she sputtered excitedly. "What if we sell tickets to the show? Profits can go to the Downtown City Animal Shelter!"

"Wow, Zoe," replied Blythe. "I love it!"

"Minka!" Zoe cried.

The little monkey scampered up to Zoe, a paintbrush behind her ear. "At your service!" she chattered.

"We've got to start making the posters right now," Zoe said. "We want the posters to be dazzling. Bright colours, big words—"

Before Zoe could even finish telling Minka what she wanted, the monkey zoomed away. Minka was just a blur as she zipped around the Littlest Pet Shop, gathering everything she would need.

About an hour later, Minka unveiled the very first poster. "What do you think? What do you think?" she asked eagerly.

"Oh, Minka!" Zoe gasped. "It's beautiful!"

Around the edges of the poster, Minka had drawn long red curtains – the kind that hang in theatres. A bright yellow spotlight shone down, with plenty of glitter so that it reflected the light, just like a real spotlight. Standing right in the middle was a drawing of...Zoe herself!

"Did I leave enough room for the letters?" Minka asked anxiously.

"Oh, definitely," Zoe assured her. "I love this design, Minka! Now for the other posters. Can you make one with PS standing in the spotlight? And one with Sam UL? And one with—"

"Let me guess: Shea Butter," Minka

said with a giggle. "Sure, Zoe."

"Awesome poster, Minka!" Blythe exclaimed as she joined them. She turned to Zoe. "Have you figured out what you want me to write?"

"How about…'*Terriers and Tiaras:* On Stage' at the top," she suggested. "You could write a different pet's name on each one. You know, PS, Shea Butter…"

"But we haven't heard back from anybody yet," Blythe reminded Zoe. "We can't call it a *Terriers and Tiaras* show without them."

"They'll be here," Zoe said confidently.

"But—" Blythe began. Then she stopped herself. "Sorry, Zoe. Whatever you say goes."

"Thanks, Blythe," Zoe said. "I'm sure we'll sell more tickets if people know they have a chance to see PS, Shea Butter and Sam UL in person!"

"And you, of course!" added Minka.

Blythe started carefully writing the words in her best handwriting. Seeing the finished poster made Zoe so happy she almost started chasing her tail in glee, just like a puppy!

Chapter 3
Stars on Set

For the next few days, the Littlest Pet Shop was buzzing with activity. There was so much noise that Zoe could barely hear herself think. But she didn't mind. With her extra-special director accessories – a folding chair and clipboard – Zoe felt like she had everything under control.

Russell and Minka had spent hours designing the set.

Zoe cocked her head as she stared at the shimmery stars that Minka had propped up against the wall. *It's a good start,* Zoe thought. *But there's something missing.*

Zoe realised that Russell and Minka were eagerly waiting to hear what she thought of their work.

"You've both done a wonderful job!" Zoe told them. "The set design couldn't possibly be better...unless..."

"What is it? What's wrong?" Russell asked anxiously.

"Oh, goodness, nothing's wrong," Zoe said. "It's just...all that gold paint...I wonder if the stars will stand out enough if they're all painted the same colour, especially to people who are sitting in the back of the lounge."

Minka scampered across the room to look at the stars from a distance. "Wow, Zoe, you're right! What are we going to do?"

"We could add some silver stars," suggested Russell.

"Perfect!" Zoe said. "Or stars in different colours…like a rainbow galaxy. I really love the shimmery paint you're using, Minka."

"Got it," Minka shouted as she rushed off to get more supplies. Zoe breathed a sigh of relief. *Problem solved!* she thought happily.

"You have great ideas," Russell said with admiration.

"How'd you get to be so good at directing?"

"That's really nice of you, Russell, but to be honest, I'm just figuring it out as I go," Zoe admitted.

"Well, you saved the set!" Russell told her.

Zoe should have been happy, but there was a strange feeling of worry tugging at her. *What if...what if there are other things I'm missing?* she wondered.

There was only one thing to do: Zoe, perched in her director's chair and feeling very official, clapped her paws together. "Attention, everyone!" she said in her best take-charge voice. "I'd like to see how your acts are coming along."

"Ooh, I love dress rehearsals!" Penny gushed.

"A dress rehearsal?" Blythe gulped.

"Don't we need costumes for that? I'm nowhere near ready!"

"Don't worry, Blythe," Zoe assured her. "It's not a dress rehearsal exactly…not yet. For now, I just want to see a preview of each act."

"Phew!" Blythe sighed. "Well, back to the sewing machine."

"Hold on," Zoe said, putting a paw on Blythe's ankle. "I was hoping you'd stay and help me. Do you want to bring your sketches? We can see how each costume matches up with each act."

"I could use some help, too," Penny spoke up. "Blythe, would you turn on my music?"

"And I need someone to introduce me," added Pepper.

"I think I can handle that," Blythe told them.

Zoe checked her clipboard. "Penny, you're up."

Penny stood very still in the middle of the stage as Blythe started the music. With a graceful motion, she brought the ribbon over her head in a wide arc – just like a rainbow. Zoe sucked in her breath as Penny started to twirl, making the ribbon dance along with her.

"Here's what I'm thinking for Penny's costume," Blythe whispered.

Zoe stole a glance at Blythe's sketch – a fluttery skirt with lace trim that perfectly matched Penny's ribbon.

"Gorgeous!"

When Penny's routine ended, Pepper took the stage. With a twinkle in her eye, Pepper pointed at her open mouth but didn't make a sound.

"That's my cue!" Blythe cleared her throat and proclaimed, "Ladies and gentlemen, it is my pleasure to introduce Pepper the mime!"

Soon all the pets were cracking up as Pepper first pretended to peel a banana, and then slipped and fell all over the stage. When she pretended the banana was chasing her, Vinnie laughed so hard *he* fell over!

"OK, Sunil, your turn!" Zoe called out. "I can't wait to find out which trick you're going to perform."

The mongoose looked at her with his big eyes. "Oh no, a magician never reveals his secrets!" he exclaimed.

"But…don't you want to practise in front of everybody?" Zoe asked.

"And ruin the surprise? Never!"

Zoe and Blythe exchanged a glance. "It's up to you," Blythe said in a quiet voice. "You're the director."

Zoe paused for a moment. *I promised that our show would be all about fun,* she thought, *and not about stress and pressure.*

"OK, Sunil," Zoe finally said. "If you want to keep your trick secret until the show, that's fine with me."

"Thanks, Zoe!" he said as he scampered back to his magic station.

Zoe peeked at her clipboard. "Let's see…who's next?"

"Me!" shouted Vinnie excitedly as he leaped in front of her. "Hit it,

Blythe!" Vinnie called.

Blythe started the music, Vinnie started dancing, and Zoe's smile started to fade. Vinnie was, well, there was only one way to put it: Vinnie was terrible! From the expression on Blythe's face, Zoe could tell she agreed.

Zoe tried to look on the bright side. *Vinnie loves to dance,* she reminded herself. *Maybe he'll let me give him some suggestions.*

"Zoe! Pay attention!" Vinnie called from the stage. "It's time for my big finish!"

"I'm watching, Vinnie!" Zoe called back encouragingly. She held her breath as Vinnie backed up, started running, took a flying leap…and crashed right into Minka's paint cans!

Bang! Clatter! Crash! Smash!

All the pets spun around to look. They found Vinnie sitting right in the middle of a rainbow puddle of paint that was spreading across the floor. The paint had splattered everywhere – even on Minka and Russell!

"Oops," Vinnie muttered. "That wasn't supposed to happen."

Just then, Mrs Twombly peeked in. "Is everything OK? I thought I heard…" she began. "Oh, gracious! Hold on – let me go and start the bathwater."

"Whoa," whispered Zoe as Mrs Twombly hurried off to get baths ready for Russell, Minka and Vinnie. Then, in a louder voice, she said, "OK, everybody, we can handle this! We'll get this mess cleaned up and then break for lunch."

Zoe hurried over to Vinnie. She held out a paw to help him up.

"That was a big finish, all right," Zoe joked, but Vinnie wasn't even able to crack a smile.

"I don't know what went wrong, Zoe," he replied glumly. "I made a mess of everything!"

"Dancing isn't easy, Vinnie," she told him. "Professional dancers have to practise for years."

"But the show is in a few days!" Vinnie said. "Maybe I should quit. I don't want to make a mess of the show, too."

Oh no, Zoe thought. *I made Vinnie feel even worse!*

"Absolutely not," Zoe said to him firmly. "We need you in the show!

With a little more practice, you'll do a great job. I can help you, too. Whatever it takes, you're going to shine."

"You really think so?" he asked.

"I know so," Zoe promised. "Now, let's get you cleaned up. We can start right away—"

Ring-a-ling!

"Hang on, Vinnie. I'll be right back," Zoe said. She poked her head through the curtain to see who had just entered the pet shop.

"PS!" Zoe shrieked. "You're here!"

Chapter 4
Friends Reunited

Philippa trailed right behind PS, pulling a large suitcase.

Zoe zoomed into the front of the Littlest Pet Shop with Blythe right behind. "We weren't expecting to see you until Thursday!" Blythe cried as she rushed forward to give Philippa a hug.

"When PS and I got your email, we decided to drive straight to Downtown City," Philippa explained. "When he heard about the show, he just wouldn't stop barking. Don't think I'm crazy, Blythe, but sometimes I feel as though our pets can understand every single word we say!"

Blythe smiled wryly. "I know exactly what you mean. Come on in and let me get you a snack. And I bet PS would like a little treat, too."

Blythe reached behind the counter and grabbed two biscuits, one for PS and one for Zoe. "I'm sure you two have a lot of catching up to do," she said.

"You bet we do," Zoe said, but to Philippa, it sounded like *yip-yip-yip-bark!*

"It's so cute how they think they can answer us, isn't it?" Philippa asked Blythe.

Zoe didn't hear Blythe's response, because she and PS were already on their way to the back of the shop. "Everybody's back here. We've been working constantly to get everything ready for the show…"

Zoe's voice trailed off as she and PS stepped through the curtain. Bubbles drifted by as Penny, Pepper and Sunil scrambled around trying to clean up the big paint spill.

"And, uh, as you can see, we're still working," Zoe finished.

Pepper glanced up from her sudsy sponge. "PS!" she howled with excitement, and that was all it took for the others to rush over to PS.

"So how's life now you're off the pageant circuit?" Penny asked eagerly.

"It's amazing!" PS told her. "Philippa is such a sweetie – a much better owner than Judi Jo. I had no idea that life could be so much fun!"

"So you don't miss being on *Terriers and Tiaras?*" asked Pepper.

PS tilted his head to the side. "I miss what it could have been," he finally said. "That's why I was so excited when I heard Zoe was organising this reunion show. At last, we can put on a show the way it's supposed to be."

"Exactly!" Zoe said. "All fun, no drama."

"No drama…but what happened

here?" PS said as he gestured to the soapy mess on the floor. "Are you working on some kind of water act?"

"Not exactly," admitted Zoe. "You could call this…technical difficulties."

"That figures," PS replied. "I've never been in a show that didn't have some big problems during set-up."

"That makes me feel so much better," Zoe told him. "I've never done something like this before. It's a lot more work than I expected."

"Don't worry, Zoe," he told her. "When Philippa read Blythe's email to me, I thought, *Only Zoe could come up with an idea this great – and pull it off!* I mean, how on earth did you even manage to reach Sam UL?"

"Reach him?" she repeated. "Well, Blythe sent an email to his owner."

"But they're spending the summer at Camp Tuff Pup," PS said. "No mobile phones, no television, and definitely no email."

"No…email?" she repeated in disbelief.

"Definitely not," PS replied.

Just then, a freshly bathed Russell burst in. "Guys!" he yelled. "The manager of the Pawza Hotel just called. They've already sold more than a hundred tickets to the show!"

This was great news – or it should have been great news – but Zoe felt like she was on the verge of a major freak-out!

Chapter 5

Stress in the Shop!

Zoe started pacing. "This is bad. Really bad. Really, really bad."

Russell looked confused. "Bad? What are you talking about?"

"PS just told me that Sam UL is at some doggy camp in the woods, so Tanya probably hasn't even got Blythe's email!" Zoe said worriedly.

All of a sudden, Russell understood what Zoe was trying to say. "Oh," he said. "That is bad."

"And if Tanya didn't get the email, she won't know to bring Sam UL here!" Zoe howled. "Which means all those posters are a lie!"

"Hang on," PS spoke up. "What do you mean?"

"I got Blythe to write '*Terriers and Tiaras:* On Stage' on every poster," groaned Zoe. "And a bunch of them have a drawing of Sam UL! But if he doesn't show up, the audience will get mad! What if they want their money back?"

I'm the director, Zoe reminded herself. *I'm in charge. And I made this mess, so it's up to me to fix it.*

"OK, here's what we're going to do," Zoe said, still working on a plan as the words tumbled out. "I'll ask Blythe to call that camp, and to email Tanya again, just in case she can get emails. Maybe Blythe can send a letter. Surely there must be a way to reach this place?"

PS opened his mouth to answer, but Zoe kept talking.

"Meanwhile, Minka can make new posters – this time without Sam UL on them," she continued. "I mean, we *will* reach him. The new posters are just a backup plan."

"That's the right attitude," PS said encouragingly.

Just then, Blythe poked her head through the curtain. "PS, Philippa says it's time to go."

"Remember – no stress! This is going

to be fun!" PS told Zoe and Russell. Then he followed Blythe to the front of the Littlest Pet Shop.

"I'm so glad PS is here," Zoe said to Russell. "We're so lucky to have a real professional."

"A professional what?" Minka asked as she scampered up to them, still dripping from her bath.

Zoe didn't waste any time telling Minka everything that had happened.

"I hate to ask this, but would you make some more posters for me?" Zoe finished. "Blythe was right. I never should've advertised Sam UL until I knew for sure he'd be in the show."

"More posters?" Minka replied, sounding worried. "I still have to repaint all those stars for the set."

"I didn't even think of that," Zoe

admitted. "Sorry, Minka. Listen – I'll make the new posters. You can focus on painting the set."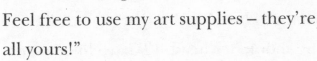

Minka breathed a sigh of relief. "Thanks, Zoe. That would be great. Feel free to use my art supplies – they're all yours!"

"Ooh, I will," Zoe replied.

"Hey, Zoe!" said a voice from behind her.

Zoe spun around to find Vinnie. "I'm ready for my first dance lesson!" he announced.

"Oh, Vinnie, I'm sorry," she said. "I have a situation that I've got to take care of immediately."

"No problem, Zoe," Vinnie said quickly.

"Maybe later?"

"Definitely," Zoe promised him. "Make sure you have your dancing shoes on!"

"Are you kidding? I never take them off!" he said. Sure enough, as Vinnie started walking away, Zoe could hear his shoes going squish-squish-squish.

Vinnie didn't wear his shoes in the bath, did he? Zoe thought doubtfully. She shook her head. *I'll have to come up with a new poster design,* she thought. *But what should it be?*

Zoe was still trying to figure out the answer to that question when Blythe approached her. "Zoe, I just realised something," Blythe began. "You didn't have a chance to show us your talent! I want to make sure I design an extra-special costume for our star director."

"Oh, Blythe, that's the least of my worries," Zoe replied with a sigh. "Right now I've got to make more posters."

"What about the posters Minka already made?"

Zoe told Blythe all her problems.

"Poor Zoe," Blythe said sympathetically. "It's not easy being in charge, is it?"

"Not really," Zoe admitted. "But I can handle it. I just wish I could draw as well as Minka."

"Hmm. I think what you need to do is put your own unique spin on them," Blythe suggested. "What if the posters focus on fundraising instead of the *Terriers and Tiaras* reunion?"

Zoe brightened right away. "I love that!" she exclaimed. "Then the audience will get a big surprise if – I mean, when – the whole cast from *Terriers and Tiaras* goes onstage. Could you write something about the animal shelter at the top?"

"Sure," Blythe replied. She grabbed a pink marker and wrote *HELP THE ANIMALS!* in giant bubble letters. Then Blythe added information about the show's date, time, location and ticket price.

Zoe felt better just seeing some words on the poster. "Thank you so much,

Blythe," she said gratefully. "What should I draw on the posters?"

"That's up to you," Blythe said. "You'll figure out something that's as creative and stylish as you are! I'd better get back to the costumes, but if you need help—"

"No, I've got it," Zoe replied quickly. She didn't want to stress Blythe out.

After Blythe left, Zoe stared at the posters. *I could draw some animals*, she thought. *But what if they don't look like animals?*

Zoe sat back as she tried to figure out what she could add to the posters. *Stars!* she thought excitedly. *I know I can handle adding some bright, colourful stars – just like the ones Minka and Russell are making!*

Then the posters will match the set, and since we have real stars like PS in our show, it all fits together perfectly!

Zoe got to work, drawing large stars.

At last, she sat back and examined her work. The posters were vibrant and fun, but her design didn't say anything about animals.

And that's when Zoe had her next brilliant idea. *I know exactly what these posters need!* she thought excitedly.

Zoe dashed over to Minka's art supplies and found a paintbox filled with pretty watercolours. She added a few drops of water to each colour. Then she took a deep breath, leaped onto the paint palette, and pranced all over each poster!

"Zoe! These posters look amazing!" Blythe squealed as she hurried over.

"Adding paw prints was genius. Let's go hang these posters around town right now."

"OK! Let's do it!" Zoe replied.

"Zoe? I think you're forgetting something," Blythe said with a giggle as she pointed at the floor.

Zoe looked down and gasped. Her paint-covered paws had left a trail of rainbow paw prints all over the floor!

"Don't worry," Blythe told her. "I'll clean the floor. You go see Mrs Twombly to wash your toes."

"You got it, Blythe,"

Zoe replied. She took a step, leaving another paw print on the floor. *Uh-oh, Zoe thought. Who knew show business could be so messy?*

Chapter 6

A Head for Heights

When Zoe's owners dropped her off
the next morning, she went straight
to Vinnie. "I'm so sorry I didn't have a
chance to help you with your routine,"
she told him. "Everything got so crazy
with PS and—"

"That's OK," he interrupted. "You're

busier than everybody else."

"I'll never be too busy for you," Zoe replied. "Let's get right to work."

But before Vinnie could even make a move, Zoe felt a small tap on her shoulder. She turned around to find Russell behind her.

"Got a minute, Zoe?" he asked.

"Well, I'm helping Vinnie," she explained. "What's up?"

"I have a problem with the set pieces," Russell told her.

Oh no! Not another problem! Zoe thought as her heart sank. "Can it wait until I finish with Vinnie?"

"Sure," he replied. "I'll watch. I can't do anything else until we figure out how to fix the set."

"No, we don't have any time to waste." Then she turned and called out, "Hold

that pose, Vinnie! I'll be
right back."

Vinnie froze in place –
with his foot high in the
air. "Whatever you say, Zoe!"
he replied, teetering back and
forth.

"No, not literally," she replied. "Just
remember where you were so we can
pick up where we left off as soon as I
get back."

"Phew!" Vinnie breathed a sigh of
relief as he put his foot on the floor.

Zoe followed Russell to the building
area. "The set looks fantastic!" she cried.
"What's the problem?"

"That's the problem," Russell replied,
as he pointed to twelve stars scattered on
the ground. "I still have to add the top
layer of stars, but I'm afraid of heights!"

"Ohhhh," Zoe said as she craned her neck to look at the top of the set. It was pretty high up. "Have you asked anyone else? What about Minka?"

Russell leaned close to Zoe and whispered, "Would you give Minka a hammer?"

"I see your point," Zoe replied. "Sunil?"

"Forget it. He's so worried that someone will see his magic trick that he's locked himself in a cupboard with it!" Russell said.

"Yikes," Zoe replied. "Well…OK. I guess I can give it a try."

"Great!" Russell exclaimed. "All you have to do is hammer each star to the one below it."

That's easy for you to say! Zoe thought.

Russell helped Zoe put on his tool belt. "Ready to go!" he told her. "When you get to the top of the ladder, I'll hoist a star up with the pulley."

Zoe gulped. "Any advice?" she asked.

"Yes," Russell replied seriously. "Don't look down! And definitely don't hammer your paw."

That's when Zoe noticed the giant bandages on Russell's paws. "Poor Russell! Are you OK?" she exclaimed.

"I will be," he replied. "I'm feeling better already – now that you're going to finish the set."

"OK," she said as she took a deep breath. "Here we go!"

Rung by rung, Zoe crawled up the ladder.

"You're a natural up there," Russell told her.

"Maybe my talent for the show could be ladder climbing," she joked.

"You mean you don't have a talent planned?" he asked in surprise.

"I – well," Zoe stammered. "It's been so busy—"

"But, Zoe!" Russell exclaimed. "You're one of the stars!"

"Don't worry, Russell," she said. "I'll do some sort of dance. I'll start practising as soon as— Whoa!"

"What's wrong?" Russell cried anxiously.

"I'm fine – just surprised!" Zoe replied. "I've reached the top already!"

"Let's get you a star!" Russell said as he began pulling on a rope to hoist one of the stars up to Zoe.

"What do I do now?" Zoe called to him.

"Just push it next to one of the stars

that's already attached to the set. Then start hammering!" Russell explained.

That sounds simple enough, Zoe thought. There was just one problem: how on earth could she manage to hold on to the star, the ladder, the hammer and the nail all at the same time?

Let's see…grab the ladder with my back paws, push the star with my nose, hammer in one front paw and nails in the other, Zoe decided.

"You OK up there?" Russell asked in a worried voice as Zoe twisted and turned on the top of the ladder.

"Never better!" Zoe replied, sounding more confident than she felt. She reached out as far as she could for the star. "Whoa-whoa!" she cried as the ladder wobbled.

As Zoe scrambled to grab hold of the

ladder, the nails flew out of her paw and hit the floor. *Ping! Ping! Ping!* Russell needed some fancy footwork to jump out of the way!

"Are you OK?" Zoe and Russell shouted at the same time.

"Don't worry about me. I'm fine," Russell said. "How are you?"

"I'm…fine," Zoe replied, taking several deep breaths. "I'm so glad you didn't get hurt. I've heard of a hailstorm, but a nailstorm?" she exclaimed. "I think we're going to need somebody to hold the ladder."

"I'd do it, but my paws are tied," Russell told Zoe. He held up his paws to show her how he'd twisted the pulley's rope through them.

"I guess we'll just have to call for help," Zoe said.

"Did somebody say help?" a new voice spoke up.

Zoe peered down at the floor and got a wonderful surprise: Shea Butter had arrived!

"Hooray! You're here!" Zoe cried with such excitement she made the ladder wobble again.

Shea Butter could tell right away what she needed to do. She raced over to the ladder and held it firmly against the wall. And that was all Zoe needed to start hammering away!

The instant she was done, Zoe scrambled down the ladder to give Shea Butter a proper welcome. Of all the pups on *Terriers and Tiaras*, Shea Butter was the most pampered. Her owner,

Cindeanna, would do just about anything to spoil her precious pet! It wasn't until Shea Butter met Zoe that she found a way to show Cindeanna how she really felt about dog shows.

"Come on, let's get you fitted for your costume," Zoe told Shea Butter.

On the way to Blythe's sewing centre, Zoe saw Vinnie – still standing right where she'd left him.

"Vinnie, I'm sorry," Zoe said in a rush. "Finishing up the set took a lot longer than I thought, and now Shea Butter's here, and—"

"Don't worry, Zoe," Vinnie said. "I think I'm doing a lot better!"

"You are?" Zoe yipped happily. "That's fantastic! I'm just going to run over to see if Blythe needs any help."

Vinnie's face fell. "I was hoping—"

"Later on, you show me what you've got, OK?" Zoe said brightly.

When Zoe and Shea Butter reached Blythe, they discovered that Cindeanna had beaten them to it.

"There you are, sweetie pie," Cindeanna cooed as she scooped Shea Butter into her arms. "Mummy's made arrangements for you to have some deluxe spa treatments after that exhausting drive!"

As soon as Cindeanna and Shea Butter left, Blythe let out a frustrated sigh.

"What's wrong?" asked Zoe.

"Cindeanna has some big ideas for Shea Butter's costume," Blythe said, gritting her teeth. "Ruffles…ribbons…

sequins…and all of it sewed by hand! Cindeanna went to a lot of trouble to bring Shea Butter here for the show. Making a spectacular costume for Shea Butter seems like the least I can do. I just wish I knew how to find the time!"

And I wish I knew how to take some of the stress away, Zoe thought anxiously. Then she realised exactly what she could do. "Blythe, I was thinking about it, and I think I should make my own costume."

"Oh, Zoe, you don't have to do that—"

"No, I want to," Zoe said quickly. "I should probably make some changes to my costume plans, too."

After all, Zoe thought, *if I haven't even figured out exactly what I want to do in the show, there's no reason to stick to my original costume idea.*

"Well…if you're sure…" Blythe said.

"I am," Zoe said firmly.

"Thanks, Zoe." Blythe finally gave in. "And if you need any help…"

"Don't worry. I'll be fine," Zoe said. Inside, though, she wasn't so sure. The show was getting closer and closer, but her to-do list was getting longer and longer.

Chapter 7
It Takes Two!

Two days before the show, Zoe called a meeting.

"Blythe, would you please open that window?" Zoe asked.

"Sure," Blythe replied as she pushed open the window, scattering a flock of pigeons that had perched there. "Sorry, pigeons," Blythe told them.

"We're so close, everybody," Zoe told her friends. "And it never would've been possible without all your hard work! There's still a lot to do, though. Today, all the performers will have their final fittings with Blythe. Then, tomorrow, we'll transport the set over to the Pawza Hotel and have a big dress rehearsal."

"Any news about Sam UL?" asked PS.

"Not yet," Zoe admitted. "I'd do anything to reach Sam UL and Tanya. I'd even try sending a message with a carrier pigeon!"

"There's still a chance Tanya got my messages, Zoe," Blythe pointed out. "After all, if it's hard to get messages to her, it's probably just as hard to get messages from her."

Zoe perked right up. "I hadn't thought

of it like that before," she said.

"There's always hope," Blythe replied. "OK, everybody, let's try on your costumes and see how they fit!"

And best of all, I finally have a little time to figure out my own act and costume, Zoe thought with relief. *Music. First, I'll have to pick out a song.* She went over to the cupboard where Mrs Twombly stored the CDs. To Zoe's surprise, she found Vinnie in there, putting all the CDs in alphabetical order.

"Vinnie!" Zoe said. "Aren't you going to try on your costume?"

"Oh…about that…" Vinnie replied. "I've decided I'm not going to be in the show."

"You're not?" Zoe exclaimed.

"I thought I could be the number one fan," he explained. "I'm just…not that good at dancing, but I am pretty great at clapping!"

A pang of guilt hit Zoe. "You can't drop out now," she told him. "Come on – show me your best moves."

"But – you've been so busy," Vinnie said. "Don't you have a million billion other, more important things to do?"

"No, I don't," she replied – and she meant it, too.

Vinnie's face lit up. "Thanks, Zoe! You're the best!" he cried.

Zoe plunked right down on the floor of the cupboard to watch.

"So I'm going to start off like this," Vinnie said, striking a pose. "Then go left-left-left, right-right-right…a big spin…then a triple twirl…"

As soon as he finished dancing, Vinnie looked at Zoe with hope in his eyes.

"Much better," she told him. She could tell that he'd changed it a lot, but it still wasn't quite right.

"Really?" Vinnie replied, looking thoughtful. "I don't know. I still feel like something's missing."

"I think it could be a little tighter," Zoe replied honestly. "And maybe you should save the triple turn for the very end."

"Oh, like a grand-finale kind of thing?" Vinnie asked.

"Exactly!" Zoe told him. "I also had a new idea for the beginning. Watch this – see what you think."

Zoe hopped up and did a few quick moves, followed by a low kick.

"Wow! That was great!" Vinnie exclaimed.

"Now we'll do it together," she encouraged him.

Vinnie took a deep breath and tried to copy Zoe's moves exactly.

"Wow, Vinnie! You're a fast learner!" she told him. "So, tell me…have you ever done a backflip before?"

"A backflip?" Vinnie asked, looking surprised. He shook his head. "I'm willing to try, though. Maybe that's the thing that my dance has been missing."

"I have an idea for a big finish – a really big finish," Zoe said, a big smile spreading across her face. "And with a little practice, I know that you'll nail it!"

Chapter 8
The Dress Rehearsal

The next evening, Zoe could hardly believe that it was time for the final rehearsal at the Pawza Hotel. The new lounge, with its glittering lights, elegant seats and highly polished stage, was so glamorous that it took Zoe's breath away.

"OK, first things first," Zoe announced.

"Let's have everybody line up in this order: PS, Penny Ling, Shea Butter, Pepper, Sunil, then me and, finally, Vinnie. But leave an extra bit of space between Pepper and Sunil. That's where Sam UL is going to stand." *I hope,* Zoe thought, as everyone shuffled into place.

"OK," Zoe continued. "So first up, we'll have everybody parade onto the stage in this order. Then we'll start the acts. And then we'll all take a bow together at the very end. So let's have everybody get backstage and run through the whole show!"

As the pets climbed the stage, Zoe stayed behind.

"Hey, Zoe," Vinnie called. "Aren't you coming with us?"

"I'm going to watch from out here," she explained.

When all the pets were assembled backstage, Zoe called, "Russell – lights out!"

The entire lounge was plunged into darkness. Then, slowly, the lights began to brighten. The curtain opened, revealing the set. Under the shining spotlights, all the shimmering stars were even more gorgeous than Zoe had imagined they would be!

"Ladies and gentlemen, boys and girls, and pets of all kinds – welcome to the first-ever *Terriers and Tiaras* Reunion Show!" Blythe announced.

Zoe settled into her seat to watch each act. PS's flashy hoop jumping was the perfect way to start the show, and Shea Butter's high-energy tumbling routine made everyone clap and cheer. But when it was Sunil's turn, he walked onto the stage – and just stood there.

"Sunil?" Zoe called from the audience. "Aren't you going to do your magic trick?"

"Not until tomorrow," he replied. "I don't want to spoil it."

Zoe tried not to sigh. "OK, if you insist," she said. "Let's move on to Vinnie."

"But I thought you're going after Sunil," Vinnie replied.

Technically, Vinnie was correct. The only problem was that Zoe still didn't have an act ready to perform. "I'm keeping it a surprise," she said quickly.

"Oh, OK." Vinnie shrugged as he

walked onto the stage. Zoe smiled proudly as she watched Vinnie dance. He was definitely doing better!

At the end of the rehearsal, Zoe was full of praise for all the pets. *And I still have the whole night to figure out my routine and make my costume,* she thought. There was just one problem: she needed to be at the Littlest Pet Shop, with access to the music and Blythe's sewing supplies.

"Blythe," Zoe said in a low voice, "you've got to convince my owners to let me sleep over at the Littlest Pet Shop tonight."

"But, Zoe, you should get a good night's sleep," Blythe replied. "Won't you rest better at home?"

"Definitely not!" Zoe said. "I've got to go over the schedule one last time. Plus, if – I mean, when – Sam UL and Tanya arrive, I want to be there to meet them."

"OK," Blythe finally agreed. "I'll call your owners as soon as we get back."

"Thanks, Blythe!" Zoe said gratefully.

It took a couple of hours to put away all the props and costumes and get everybody back to the Littlest Pet Shop for their owners to collect them. By the time the last pet had been picked up, it was already past Zoe's bedtime – and she was feeling sleepier than ever.

It won't take too long to figure out my act, she tried to tell herself. *I just have to pick out a song…work on my dance moves…find some fabric…make a costume…*

Zoe rubbed a paw across her eyes as she yawned again.

This fabric looks nice, she thought as

she touched a beautiful bolt of velvet. *It's so soft. Maybe I'll just sit here for a minute…and then I'll…*

But as soon as Zoe laid her head on the cosy, cushiony velvet, she fell fast asleep.

Chapter 9
Wake-Up Call

Zoe stretched and smiled, still fast asleep. In her dream, her costume was gorgeous and her performance was perfect. The entire show was an enormous success!

"Zoe! Zoe! Wake up!"

Someone was shaking her shoulders.

Zoe opened her eyes and blinked. She

looked up to see all her closest friends gathered around.

"Why did you sleep in the workshop?" Blythe asked in concern.

Why did I sleep in the workshop? Zoe wondered sleepily. *I was making my costume…wait…did I make my costume?*

Then it all came flooding back. Zoe gasped in horror. She'd fallen asleep before choreographing her dance routine and making her costume…

"Oh no!" Zoe howled. "I'm not ready!"

"Not ready?" Russell asked, looking confused. "But, Zoe, you've been working like a dog for days."

Zoe paced frantically. "Everything's ruined – everything!" she sobbed. "Sam UL never showed up, and now I can't be in the show, either!"

"What on earth are you talking about?"

Blythe asked. "Of course you'll be in the show, Zoe—"

"But I don't have a talent to perform," she explained miserably. "There was always something more important to take care of. I don't even have a costume!"

At last, Zoe's big secret was out.

"No Sam UL. No Zoe. How can we call it a *Terriers and Tiaras* show if half the cast is missing?" Zoe continued. "The whole show is falling apart…and it's all my fault!"

"Yes…I guess it is your fault," Blythe said in a voice that made everyone turn to look at her. "If you hadn't had such a wonderful idea—"

"If you hadn't emailed my owner," Shea Butter spoke up.

"If you hadn't drawn the new posters," added Minka.

"And finished building the set," Russell said.

"And told me to focus on making everyone else's costumes instead of yours," continued Blythe.

"And helped me rehearse," Penny said.

"And taught me to dance," said Vinnie.

"There wouldn't be a show at all," Blythe finished. "If you're not ready to perform in the show, it's only because you've been working so hard to help everybody else."

"It's very sweet of you to say that, Blythe, but the truth is, I couldn't pull it off," Zoe said. "It was all just too much for me."

"No way, Zoe," Blythe said firmly. "You've worked too hard to give up now! We still have an hour. That's plenty of time for me to whip up a quick costume for you."

"But, Blythe, I don't even need a costume," Zoe said. "I don't have an act."

"Yes, you do," Vinnie announced. He held out a hand to Zoe. "You'll be dancing with me."

"Like…a *pas de deux*?" Zoe asked.

Vinnie nodded enthusiastically. "Yeah! I bet you know the routine by heart already. You helped me practise it for hours."

"Backflips *are* one of my specialities," Zoe said.

Blythe scrambled to her feet. "If you're dancing with Vinnie, I know just what to make for your costume!" she cried excitedly.

Hope spiralled through Zoe's heart. Maybe, just maybe, everything was going to work out!

"Thank you!" she cried. "I really do have the best friends ever!"

"You can thank us later," Blythe teased her with a big smile. "But right now, you'd better start practising!"

Zoe and Vinnie spent the next hour changing his solo dance into a routine that was perfect for two. All the while, Blythe's sewing machine was going

clackity-clackity-clack. It almost sounded like the machine was keeping time with the music.

"Finished!" Blythe finally cried.

As Blythe helped Zoe into her beautiful new costume, Zoe closed her eyes.

"Well?" Blythe asked. "What do you think?"

Zoe took a step towards the mirror and opened her eyes. "Oh, Blythe," she whispered. "It's perfect! Thank you, thank you, thank you!"

The bright red skirt Blythe had whipped up for Zoe had an extra layer of flouncy ruffles, plus dozens of sequins scattered around it. Matching ribbon roses for Zoe to wear behind her ears added the perfect finishing touch.

Just then, Mrs Twombly poked her head into Day Camp. "Oh, Zoe, don't you look adorable!" she cooed. "Blythe, you've truly outdone yourself. I know all the pets would thank you if they could!"

Blythe and Zoe exchanged a secret smile. Mrs Twombly would never understand just how hard all the pets had worked, too.

"Anyway, I was just popping in to see if everyone was ready," Mrs Twombly continued. Blythe's eyes twinkled. "Time to load up the van and head over to the Pawza Hotel. It's showtime!"

Chapter 10
Time to Shine!

Standing behind the heavy velvet curtain on stage, Zoe could hear muffled voices chatting and laughing as the audience members found their seats. *I guess it's time to face the truth,* Zoe thought sadly. *Sam UL didn't make it.*

"It's OK, Pepper," Zoe said. "You can

move forward. Sam UL isn't coming."

"Says who?" someone asked.

Zoe spun around to
see Sam UL standing
right behind her! "But
– what..." Zoe sputtered.
"I thought – Sam UL! You
made it!"

The shaggy brown Brussels Griffon
chuckled. "You didn't really think I'd
miss the first-ever *Terriers and Tiaras*
reunion show, did you?"

"PS told us that you were completely
unreachable," Zoe explained. "I didn't
know if you even got our messages."

"I almost didn't," he replied.

"So how did you find out about the
show?" Zoe asked.

"You'll never believe it," Sam UL
began. "Yesterday afternoon, a flock of

pigeons flew up to the camp to tell me. They'd heard about it from their cousins who live right here!"

Zoe remembered the flock of pigeons perched on the windowsill of the Littlest Pet Shop. *I made a joke about carrier pigeons,* she thought, *but I never expected them to follow through!*

"I managed to get Tanya to follow me into the computer room, and while she was there, she couldn't help but check her emails!" Sam UL continued. "The two of us drove all night. It gave me plenty of time to work on my Barking Boot Camp routine!"

Just then, Blythe appeared. "You made it!" she whispered happily as she patted Sam's head. "Everybody ready? The lights will dim in one minute."

Zoe showed Sam UL where to stand.

"You'll follow Pepper, first in the parade, then for your talent," she explained. "I wish we had time to practise, but—"

"Don't worry, Zoe," Sam UL interrupted her with a grin. "I'm a professional!"

"Ladies and gentlemen, boys and girls, pets of all kinds – welcome to the *Terriers and Tiaras* Reunion Show!" Blythe announced.

With a sudden whoosh, the curtain opened. Zoe stood straighter. This was it: their cue.

At the end of the Pet Parade, Zoe found herself backstage. There wasn't enough room for everybody in the wings, but if Zoe scrunched against the wall, there was just enough space to watch each performance. Zoe's heart swelled with pride as she watched her friends perform. Every act was unique and wonderful in its own way…just like each of Zoe's pals.

Sam UL marched onto the stage and wowed the crowd with his tough-guy boot camp drills. *This is why it was so important for Sam UL to be here,* Zoe thought happily. *It really wouldn't have been the same without him.*

When Sunil took the stage, Zoe realised how glad she was that he had insisted on keeping his act a secret – because she was more surprised than anyone when he somehow made paw-print-shaped confetti rain down on the entire audience!

As Sunil took a bow, Vinnie joined Zoe in the wings. That could only mean one thing: their *pas de deux* was next!

When the first notes of their song drifted through the air, Zoe and Vinnie pranced onto the stage. Zoe could tell that she and Vinnie were dancing in perfect unison. Zoe stepped back so that Vinnie could show off the fancy footwork they'd practised. She held her breath as she watched him dance – but Vinnie didn't miss a beat! The crowd was cheering as he stepped back for Zoe's mini solo.

With the spotlight – and all eyes – on her, Zoe started dancing with her heart and soul. A double dip, a triple twirl, the feel of her ruffly skirt fluttering with every move she made… Zoe was loving it! And so was the audience. That's when she realised that the real glory of performing didn't come from starring in the spotlight. It came from bringing joy to everyone watching.

Right on cue, Vinnie moved next to Zoe for their big finish. They glanced at each other and exchanged a quick nod before... With a tremendous leap into the air, both Zoe and Vinnie pulled off two perfect backflips – at the exact same time! The crowd went wild. It was the perfect ending to the perfect show.

"I think we figured out what my routine was missing, Zoe," Vinnie said.

"What's that?" Zoe asked.

"You!" he replied.

As the rest of the pets filed onto the stage, Zoe felt a sudden pang of sadness. *I don't want it to end,* she thought.

After the performers took their bow, Minka, Russell and Blythe joined them on stage to get some credit for all the fine work they'd done. Then something completely unexpected happened. With a wave and a whistle, Blythe beckoned to someone offstage.

Everyone watched in surprise as workers from the animal shelter walked on. Each one escorted an animal who Zoe had never seen before: cute cats, roly-poly pups – even a bunny and some birds.

Blythe stepped over to the microphone. "Friends, I have a big announcement to make!" she said with an enormous smile. "All profits from tonight's show have been donated to the Downtown City Animal Shelter.

Tonight, all these pets have had their food and medical care paid for. That means they're ready to be adopted! So if anyone is looking for a furry friend to join your family, we have adoption applications for you to fill out, and some very special pets who'd love to meet you. Thank you all for your support, and have a great night!"

From centre stage, Zoe watched as people hurried forward to get adoption applications.

Blythe crossed the stage and knelt beside Zoe. "This is all thanks to you," she said in a low voice. "From putting on the show to donating to the animal shelter…it couldn't have happened without you."

"Oh, Blythe," Zoe said, feeling proud, but a little embarrassed. "It was all of us –

everybody worked hard to make this happen."

"But it was all your idea," Blythe told her as she leaned down to give Zoe a giant hug. "And no one worked harder than you."

And that made Zoe really feel like a star!

The End

Read on for a sneak peek
of the next exciting
Littlest Pet Shop adventure,

Project Funway

Bzzz. Bzzz. Bzzz.

Blythe Baxter pulled the pillow over
her head.

Bzzz. Bzzz. Bzzz.

What was that buzzing noise?

It wasn't the alarm clock. Today was
Saturday; Blythe could sleep in as late as
she wanted.

So what was it?

That's when Blythe noticed her phone,
all lit up and buzzing like crazy. The clock
on her desk read 2:53 a.m.

Who's calling me in the middle of the night? She pressed the answer button and mumbled, "Hello?"

"Blythe, darling, how are you?"

Blythe sat up straighter, completely wide awake. There was no mistaking that voice – it was the one and only Mona Autumn, publisher of the world-famous fashion magazine Tres Blasé.

Blythe had been in awe of her ever since she'd sketched her very first fashion design.

Everybody knew that Blythe loved fashion. But what people didn't know was that she also had a top-secret ability. She could communicate with animals! Blythe and the pets at the Littlest Pet Shop had so many amazing adventures together – including a recent trip to the international Pet Fashion Expo, where

Russell the hedgehog had been photographed for Tres Blasé!

"I'm calling from Paris with the most fabulous news," Mona said briskly. "Our latest issue of Tres Blasé – yes, that's right, the one with you and your prickly pet – has sold more than half a million copies!"

"Half a million copies?" Blythe repeated, in shock.

"And still selling!" Mona crowed. "Needless to say, everyone's thrilled."

"I'm so—" Blythe started, but Mona kept talking.

"And the public! The public is beyond thrilled! What they want, Blythe, is more. More Blythe Style, more fashion hedgehog, more Tres Blasé! That's where you come in. We want you and Russell as the headline stars for a very special event being held in Paris in ten days!"

"A fashion show?" Blythe was so excited her voice sounded all squeaky.

"Better," Mona declared. "A fashion show at the first-ever Everyday Hero Awards, on the runway at Paris airport!"

"Mona, I'm honoured," Blythe said.

"Yes, of course you are," Mona replied. "All eyes will be on you!"

Blythe grabbed her notebook and a pen. "Which fashions should I bring for the show?" she asked.

"Bring? No, no, no – you mean design," Mona corrected her. "We want all-new designs debuted here, Blythe. I want you to think *daring and dramatic* for your designs. Just like the heroes we'll be honouring."

"I'm sorry – did you say all-new designs?" she repeated. "For a show that's in two weeks?"

"Not two weeks. Ten days," Mona said. "I'm sure you can come up with at least seven new designs by then."

"Um, yes, of course," Blythe said. But inside, she was about ten seconds away from panicking! Mona was asking for a lot.

"Since you'll be the only designer for this show, you'll get to make all the big decisions – from sets and lights to models—"

"You mean I can choose the pet models, all by myself?"

"Exactly," replied Mona. "I'll call back soon to finalise all the details. Be ready to wow me, Blythe! Ciao!"

And just like that, Mona hung up.

"Bye, Mona," Blythe whispered. Then she sat bolt upright in bed. Suddenly she felt very awake. She had an international fashion show to prepare for. There wasn't a moment to lose!

The next morning, Blythe's dad, Roger, put on his pilot uniform and went to the kitchen to make some coffee. He was surprised to see that Blythe was already there.

"What day is it?" Roger asked. "I could've sworn it was Saturday—"

"It is Saturday, Dad," Blythe replied. "You are never going to believe the phone call I got!" She quickly told him everything.

"I know it's pretty last-minute, but can you take the pets and me to Paris in ten days?" Blythe asked.

"Are you kidding?" Roger exclaimed. "It will be an honour to fly you to Paris!"

"Thank you so much!" Though she missed him when he had to travel for work, there were a lot of perks to having a pilot for a father. And with the fully-equipped Pet Jet at their service, Blythe and her pals from the Littlest Pet Shop could always travel in style.

"I can't wait to tell the pets about the trip! I know they'll be so excited—"

Too late Blythe realized what she'd said. "I mean, their owners will be so excited," she quickly corrected herself. Not even Blythe's dad knew that she could communicate with animals. Luckily, though, he didn't seem to notice her slip.

Read
Project Funway
to find out what happens next!

Turn the page for a special surprise from Blythe!

Welcome!

Hey, Pet Shop friends,
My pet pals and I have put together
some fantastic activity pages for you!

Turn the page to
discover all
sorts of fun
puzzles and
word games.

We hope you
enjoy it. See you
next time at the
Littlest Pet Shop!

Love,
Blythe
X

Wordsearch

Six words from the *Terriers and Tiaras On Stage* story
are hidden in this grid. Can you find them all?

T	E	R	R	I	E	R	S
I	C	V	H	U	L	F	B
A	A	I	I	F	O	A	L
R	T	A	W	N	P	P	Y
A	W	M	I	Y	N	P	T
S	A	N	O	B	K	I	H
O	L	Z	C	N	E	U	E
L	K	Z	O	E	T	E	R

TERRIERS   **TIARAS**   **VINNIE**

ZOE   **BLYTHE**   **CATWALK**

Minka's Masterpiece

Minka has drawn a fabulous picture of Zoe! Can you recreate it? Copy each square into the grid below.

Cast List

Ever thought about putting on a show of your own? Make a list of all your friends and the parts they would play!

Accessorisin'

Can you match these pets with their favourite item?
Draw a line to connect each one.

All about You!

What makes you tick? Fill in these pages with all your favourite facts about yourself.

Draw a picture of yourself in this frame! When you are done, add your name at the bottom.

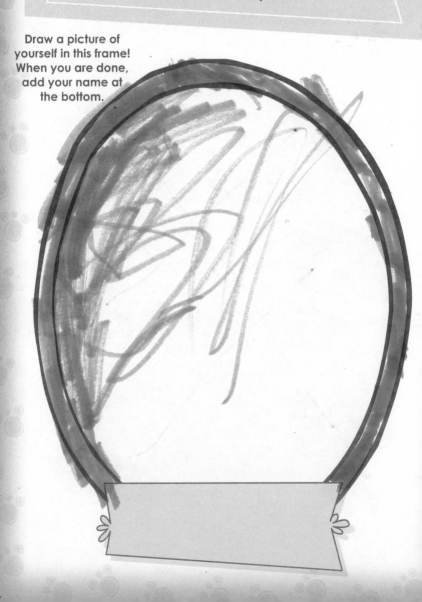

I am from...

Age

_____

_____

My Top 5 Favourite
Books Are...

1 _____
2 _____
3 _____
4 _____
5 _____

My Top 5 Favourite
Foods Are...

1 _____
2 _____
3 _____
4 _____
5 _____

When I grow up
I want to be...

_____
_____
_____
_____
_____

Dance Moves

How many different kinds of dance can you name?
Write them here, then ask a friend to see what they got.

ballets

Doggy Diva

Zoe dreams of being on the catwalk! Design a new hairdo and tail for her to strut her stuff on the runway.

Purple Power

Look around your house and see how many purple
things you can find. Write them all down on these pages!

Amazing Maze

Can you help Zoe find her way through this maze to be reunited with her sister Gail?

FINISH

START

Odd Dog Out

One of these pictures of Zoe is different from the others.
Can you spot which one?

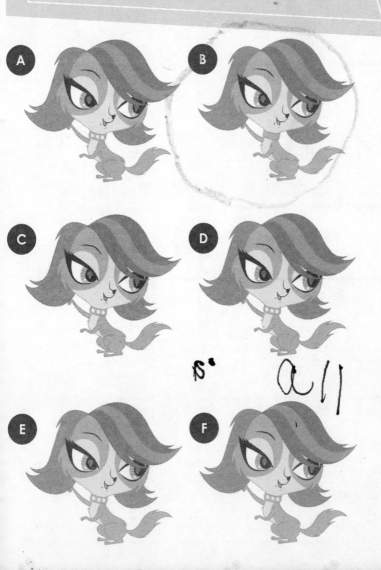